Santa's Nav

By

Mary J Lamming-Stone

M J C Lamming-Stone- Copyright ©2019

Dedication

Many thanks to the creative writing
group for encouraging me.

G. Goddard for proof reading.

Photos by M. Lamming-Stone

Additional Illustrations by

L. Collins

'Out and away across the horizon
he flew

Over the treetops around the
spire, along the river

Higher and higher.

Santa and Rudolf, Blitzen and co

Follow the Santa Nav wherever it
goes.'

Contents

What's Santa up to?

Blitzen had just had her fur waved and her hooves trimmed.

She wanted a girls night out really, but it was business as usual.

When was she to have a night off!!!

Blooming presents! did the kids really know the effort it takes. All that flying around, the blizzards, the heat, and now no chimneys!! She wanted excitement, a night off.

Maybe she could fool Santa, for just one night. He had a new toy himself. A Santa Nav. He didn't need her expertise anyhow.

Rudolf had the looks but no brain. He'd be ok without her. Wouldn't he!?

So this Xmas night Blitzen asked Allegra to take her place. They were cousins and she was a good flyer learning the ropes. Santa would never notice.

Santa

Santa had been around for centuries. He'd always looked old but of course he wasn't really.

He wasn't quite sure how he got the job in the first place, but he was born to it. He loved making children happy.

Santa often reflected on how amazing it was that he could reach all of the children on Christmas Eve, but of late he was helped by Elf no 1 quite a bit, as he had lots of energy and great ideas. His secret was having a great team of reindeer. This year he decided to have some new blood in the team to make sure that they could cover all of the country's super quick. Added to which his new 'super dooper' sparkle eco sleigh and new Santa Nav would be unsurpassed.

Santa normally had a very ordinary life with Doreen and the kids. He went shopping like

we all do, he had breakfast, lunch and dinner.
But unlike you and me he had a special job.
He was the man in charge of the magical
reindeer and MD of the Santa factory, run by
the elves and floor managed by the Mrs.
It was a busy life. A lot of research went into
the toys. But it was getting more of a
challenge.
Elf no 1 was on to it with his team of helpers,
what they couldn't make they sourced from
elsewhere and between you and me they
asked help from others who knew the children
better. But that's a secret!
Santa was getting older now, so he was glad
of help.
He was a very jolly person mostly.
He wondered how the trip this year would go

Doreen

Doreen loved Santa.

She was a bit younger than him but they had been together for ages. She loved looking after Santa and helping out in the toy factory. Doreen was a perfect Mrs Santa, she was smart and homely, kind and generous. She cared for all the family, she helped the elves and her favourite animal was the reindeer, especially the kids.

She nurtured them from babies.

Doreen was very fond of Allegra, who was very lovable and cute, but they were all special.

She hoped Santa would take Allegra on his trip this year, as she was now old enough to go.

Doreen knew it would be an exciting trip this year, but different and a bit more stressful with the new contraption.

Santa could get worried, but he usually got by, with a little help from his elf friends.

She had a new Imp phone so she could keep in touch and follow Santa on his journey.

Doreen was planning a nice feast for Christmas day. Everyone would be invited and then Santa would have a good rest before they went on holiday.

She would enjoy looking at the possible destinations.

She needed sun sea and sand after all of the snow and ice she saw every day.

Elf No 1

Elf no one had been helping Santa for years now, but he had a hankering for a bit more excitement!

He'd spotted the most amazing motorbike on his Imp pad.

It was red and white with flame designs on it.

And the snow guards were v shaped like stars.

He would do anything to get one of those.

He thought it could be adapted to make a fantastic sleigh bike and perfect for Santa's helper to have.

It would be very nippy and reach the awkward places where Santa's big sleigh had a few problems.

He had it in mind to mention this to Santa in the new year, so that all could be prepared for next year if Santa agreed.

He'd had a go on a snow bike before, when other elves came to visit but of course theirs didn't look so Christmassy or exciting as his would. It would be adapted in the workshop by the mechanic elves who were very clever.
It would be re sprayed and sparkled, and its tank converted to use eco sparkle oil.
This excitement and his joy of Christmas filled his head and made him feel very happy.

On Christmas Eve

Santa was grumbling, he wanted the sleigh packed just right. He had a new outfit on and it was a bit scratchy!! It didn't fit perfectly either. It was a bit smaller than the old one, he thought! But between you and me he'd tried a few too many of Mrs Santa's mince pies!

He opened the amazing delivery of his Santa Nav and secured it to his new Nav Sleigh.

He sat looking at it, pushed a few buttons and hey presto there was his earth view and his circumnavigation route around the world, all prepared. He only had to press the 'Go' button.

He hadn't tried it out further than a little village called Bidavon and that was last summer, and it worked fine then.

The elves gathered round and encouraged
him with oohs and ahs and words like
awesome, or amazing.
Things would be so easy now. No getting lost.
No real need of Blitzen; who could be
temperamental.

The time came for the reindeer to saddle up.
All were in order of importance. The sparkle
dust hay that helped them on their way was in
their nose bags.

Santa sat at his controls and with excitement pressed Go!!!

Whoosh! they went into the frosty night sky, Santa could see where they were on his ten inch screen and Mrs Santa could follow them at home on her Imp phone. She was busy making the Xmas cake.

Santa loved his view from the sleigh, there was nothing quite like it.

He had updated to the new deluxe model which had extra flashy lights along the side, silver skis and seatbelts.

He had asked for cruise control and an 'eco route', so the journey could be completed sooner.

He would be back home for dinner with the wife and the turkey!

Soon, it was time for a break.

They pulled up on a lovely iceberg. The reindeer topped up on sparkle hay and crystal water.

Santa had a quick bite of his packed lunch.

Yum. Pickled onion sandwiches with sparkle crisps.

Rudolf was impatient and was getting bored. He wanted to get going so he pressed the 'Go' button on the Santa Nav screen.

Wooo!

The route finder went crazy!!
It shouted at Santa!!!
It spoke in a weird accent.
The sleigh somersaulted and twisted in the air. It looped the loop!
There was Santa holding on to his seat belt and his Santa Nav for dear life!!
The reindeer broke out of their harness and started to go in all different directions and the sleigh started to zig zag most strangely.

Santa shouted at the Santa Nav.

'Get me back on my eco setting this minute'
he commanded. But the Santa Nav had a
mind of its own
'Turn left immediately then right at the Eiger!!!
'What!?
"We are not going anywhere near the Eiger,"
said Santa in complete frustration and
despair.

Santa was not in control anymore!

He regretted getting the Santa Nav that Mrs
Santa had recommended. He should have
stuck to the tried and tested method; he
should have trusted Blitzen! Oh well, at least
she's somewhere around. He'd whistle to her
and she'd come galloping to him as usual.
He whistled once. No Blitzen! He whistled
twice still no Blitzen. She must have gone off
course!

Santa spied Rudolf recovering from the upset,
and, smoothing down his soft coat, checked

his harness was looking ok and sparkly after the unexpected sleigh antics.

'Where's Blitzen, Rudolf?" said Santa.

Rudolf said he hadn't seen her for ages. He knew that she'd swapped herself for Allegra and she didn't want to be found out.

He wasn't going to tell.

Santa started to worry about Blitzen. He needed her, she was only a baby reindeer when they had first met, he'd taught her the way, and she'd learned the ropes better than anyone before. She was to be relied on.

Only Blitzen could help them and get them back on course.

Ok let's try again said Santa!!

He typed in the next address on his schedule. Great, somewhere hot at last. He needed a bit of sun, surf, and sand. We're off to Oz he shouted ecstatically!

Up, up, and a little to the left they flew, over the hill tops, across the ocean, over the chimneys and the forests.
Err! Said Santa scratching his head, umm! This doesn't look like Australia. It's not hot! It's wet and cold.

Real Santa

A little village came into sight. It had a big old bridge and a large field.

"I remember this ", said Santa.

Lots of space to land, lots of old chimneys, and possibly lots of children Looks good but not quite the plan.

It was night time, and the Santa loved to sneak into the church on his way past. It was cold and chilly but this year he saw lots of decorated trees inside!
It was beautiful and it reminded him of home.

The village lights twinkled out across the big river. Santa didn't want to be too obvious, so he said they'd land across the field away from the bridge. He forgot he was lit up like a Christmas tree.

Within minutes people were swarming to his sleigh. Mums and dads, children, grannies and grandads, all were gathered round, flashing their torches excitedly.

They were offering Santa money and they asked for sweets. Santa ferreted around about and found a big bag of chocolate reindeer coins. He threw them out to the crowd. They were thrilled.

The reindeer proved to be the greatest attraction. The children hadn't seen them before. The reindeer liked the attention. Particularly Ray, who was a bit vain.

One child came up to Santa.

"You are not the usual one we get around here are you", he said.

He plays loud music and his sleigh is on a lorry.

"No! I'm the 'Real' Santa", Santa said. "Ho, ho, ho", and he beamed.

Wow!! Are you really Santa?

"Yes I am, and these are my flying reindeer".

The boy rushed off to tell his mum.
Santa was having a fantastic time. But he knew the time was pressing on.
He told the crowd that he had to go now but he'd be back next year.
He hoped his sleigh would take off again!

Jacks mum was impressed with the new Santa. she told Jack that this Santa looked very real indeed. But she knew it wasn't. It couldn't be.
Santa pressed Go. Nothing happened!! Oh no!
The reindeer tugged at the sleigh, nothing moved. They huffed and puffed." It's way too heavy ", said Rudolf. Even the sparkle dust didn't help.
"What shall we do? "said Santa desperately.

Where's Blitzen. He whistled!! Nothing! Where was she?

Allegra loved gadgets and she'd had a sneaky look at the new sleigh. She had an idea. Had Santa spotted the thrusters that gave an extra lift in difficult situations. Should she remind Santa about it? Yes, maybe she should. She wanted to move up the ranks.

"Err Santa! "Yes," said Santa. "What do you want? "Santa said grumpily.

"Well", she said, "how about that button"!

"Which one" said Santa.

That red one? "This red one", said Santa and pushed it impatiently. What could she know about it!!!?

The sleigh shot up vertically into the air!!! The poor reindeer were in shock! They lagged behind somewhat.

Well it seemed to work, and Santa was totally amazed. Wow!!! What an amazing sleigh this is, vertical lift and thrust as well as speed.

He was Impressed with this new little upstart Allegra. She seemed quite clever after all.

Mrs Santa

Mrs Santa, Doreen to Santa and the kids, put down her big wooden spoon. She'd just mixed up the Christmas cake and added the sultanas and the candied fruit. She'd been watching the Imp phone with great interest. What was going on?

The picture had been very clear up till now. She had seen the sky at night, the passing stars twinkling as they flew.

She was following Santa's journey as planned.

But now something looked very strange. Something very furry came into view, what was it?

Oh my goodness! Now she could see into Rudolf's eyes, then up his nose!!! Not nice!

Then she saw Santa. He was in a bit of a pickle. His legs were in the air, and he was shouting and flailing around.

She heard a few rude words as well.

Had Santa's Navigation system come adrift! Oh my days! It must have!

"Doreen can you see us" came a familiar booming voice across the Nav speaker! Have you seen Blitzen? He said in desperation.

She's not here and I need her to help us.

Strangely Mrs Santa wondered why Blitzen was leisurely grazing outside! She thought it wasn't like Santa to leave her behind.

"Err yes dear ", she said hesitantly. She's here, I think. Do you want a word!!

Well Santa got redder in the face and said some more rude words.

Just as he was about to explode the screen went dead!! No sound no picture!!

"Well "said Doreen, I'd best get on with the mince pies. She knew he'd find a way to get home.

Blitzen was munching happily.
"Guess Santa is halfway through the trip by now ", she said to herself.
She hated to admit it but she was missing the best bits of the trip. She liked flying and being important. She liked being Santa's no 1 guide really.
Never mind she'd be there next year, wouldn't she!
He won't notice her missing, not with his new contraption.

Sun, sea and Santa

Finally, Santa appeared to be getting the hang of the Santa Nav after a few little teething problems.
They made up time and he felt more confident with Allegra by his side.

As the sleigh flew it got gradually lighter and the bags of presents got less and less. The chief no 1 Elf, that stacked the sleigh and counted the presents felt a relief that they were getting through most of the toy requests from all of the children.

How they had changed over the years.

No one wanted paints or books anymore they usually wanted cell phones, X Boxes or what they called tablets!! Elves couldn't make these.

Some teddies were still asked for and a few dolls, but everything was changing just like Santa's sleigh.

Elf no 1 sat down in his leather comfy seat and did up his seat belt. Time to relax till they reached the next stop.

The slay hovered over the deep blue sea, they could see coloured fish under the water and coral swaying. The sun was shining, and it was very hot indeed! Santa liked to visit tropical countries, he always holidayed abroad these days. Mrs Santa would be no doubt looking at her many catalogues just as soon as the Xmas season was over!

Santa took off his coat leaving his silky red Santa T shirt on view. It was a good job he had some festive shorts on, he thought. The reindeer were glad they had magic powers, and in a flash their coats became lighter and cooler to cope with the heat.

On the beach were coconuts and tables laid out, but it was early so no one was around to see them. Santa said to be quick, put the presents on the beach for the local children to find. They would be up and about in no time. They climbed down over the thrusters and sparkly skis, and they made a line to carry the bags of toys over the deep sand onto a big rock in the middle of the golden beach. Each toy had a name on it and Santa knew all of the children.

Back on the sleigh Santa used his hover mode to stay near but high up to watch the children's faces when they saw the gifts. They were beaming and dancing around with delight. He had the best job in the universe he thought.

Nosey Rudolf

The sea seemed endless, it seemed to blend into the sky until it got darker and they came over the land once more. A long, wide, snaking river came in sight and lots of big bridges, barges and ships.

This time the sleigh stopped on a very large roof! All around were chimneys and domes. Lots of windows and doors.

"Now how did I get in last year?' said Santa. He opened a small hatch in a big chimney and squeezed in his fat tummy. He pulled his large sack in after him.

Rudolf; who was a bit nosey, in more ways than one, could not stop himself from taking a peek through the hatch to see what was through it.

He saw Santa eating mince pies and putting carrots in his pocket. He even saw him drinking something!

Santa carefully placed toys at the foot of the children's beds.
The floor- boards were creaky so he had to go on tip toe.

"I wonder who they are "said Rudolf. They must be very rich to live in such a grand palace.

Santa sprinkled silver dust around the fireplace to prove he'd been there and he left a 'thank you' note for the nice food.

"Rudolf you are in luck ", said Santa! I've got carrots for you from the children. Isn't it nice when they think of us.

Rudolf shared his carrot with Allegra as she had saved the day! and Santa put some aside for later on.

Santa said that these children were very lucky and important.
They believed in him and he liked that.

George would be King one day and his sister Charlotte was a princess.

Off they went again. They circled Big Ben and flew over the Houses of Parliament, over Middle Temple, waived at the barristers in their wigs, and out along the embankment.

Oops!

They zoomed over the white cliffs of Dover and spotted the Arc de Triomphe. Into Spain they hovered over the big cathedral in Barcelona. They descended onto flat roofs and left a stocking or two, they zoomed over the Alps, whooshed over Norway and Sweden; where it was very snowy and cold. They spotted the Northern Lights over Lapland, which they saw quite often, and then they were all set for home.

Santa stroked his beard, he wasn't quite sure what rating he'd give the new Santa Nav, it was very good, but it had its glitches. If it hadn't been for Allegra they wouldn't have got the deliveries done and there would be lots of disappointed children.

Last lap now, Santa thought. Soon I'll be home with Doreen.

He was so happy, that he ate his last sandwich and his last cup of hot chocolate.

One of the elves came rushing up to him. "We've just found three undelivered stockings!!! What shall we do?"

Santa looked at the teddy who looked at him and gave him a wink.

"Oh dear that will never do" he said. Nothing for it but well have to return as fast as lightning. Warp speed if possible~"
Santa had noticed a red button on his new sleigh! In the handbook there was a warning.

Only press if you have to go very, very fast, do seatbelts up and hold onto your hats!

Oh well maybe this was the opportunity to try it out.

OK, said Santa, "Seatbelts on if you want to stay with me, this could be a bumpy ride!!"

Nothing happened! Better do it again, said Santa, but just as he was mid word----
Yikes!!! They rocketed, zoomed and swerved. Santa could hardly see any clouds, houses, or hills, they were going so fast. He rocked from side to side as the reindeer swerved to avoid steeples, hills, houses and blocks of flats!!

After what seemed like no time at all, the Sleigh came to a hovering halt in mid-air!!

Over a steeple in a small village

Jane, her Rabbit, and her Dad were scanning the night sky for Santa. She had not liked the idea of Santa coming down their chimney!! Anyhow he wouldn't fit!

Her dad said that was fine Santa would find a way to leave her a present.

She was sure she'd be on his list as she'd been kind and polite, mostly! She'd tried anyhow.

Suddenly she saw a silver streak flash across the sky, right across the big picture window. They both stared in disbelief!!!!

Wow!!! That was Santa and the reindeer, no question.

Mum had gone to church, but Dad was looking after his only child, on Xmas Eve.

The little church of St Helena's was lit up. it's pretty coloured windows shining out into the darkness, and the trees in the churchyard were covered in fairy lights. Outside there was a sleigh and a Santa in it, but not the real one.

The bells were starting to ring out and all of the people were gathering to sing Christmas carols.

Dad said it was time to go to sleep now. No presents if you were still awake.

Jane was a bit tired. So, she pretended to shut her eyes.

It was not long before she was really asleep.

In the distance Santa's sleigh was hovering. No one was about. Everyone was inside the church.

They settled in the dusky churchyard and unloaded a big hamper for people who didn't have presents. Santa took his bag of three stockings. One for Jane, and the other two for two neighbours in the big house.

As if by magic he was eating the mince pies in Janes' front room and collecting the carrots for the reindeer. A glass of whisky was a great treat for Santa, but he really shouldn't have drunk it!! Not when in charge of his new sleigh.

Quickly he went over to the big house, he left his sack in the big dining room by the big tree and gave a quick wave to the horses in the stable, he told them not to breathe a word.

Santa got back to the sleigh in double quick time. Out of the church came a woman dressed in a very strange way!! I think they call them priests said Allegra. They dress up on special days. She was wearing a lovely red old-fashioned St Nicholas, bishop type outfit, a bit like a tunic. Not like what Santa wears now.

She spotted real Santa and gave him a wink and a wave. She'd seen him before when he was delivering gifts, but she always kept it a secret. The Vicar was grateful that Santa made people happy.

The sleigh took off slowly and soared above the square tower of the pretty little church, it circled once, just in time to hear the organ playing loudly. Over the big house with its big gates and away over the fields and the river Avon.

By Santa's side

Allegra was sitting by Santa's side
"So where is Blitzen" said Santa" feeling a bit
sad.
"Oh dear "said Allegra, "I don't like to tell tales,
but I can't lie to you Santa can I?" "Err no ",
said Santa, "I will understand, just spill the
beans and I'll try to help". "Ok ", Allegra said.
"Well between you and me I, think she's past
it, she wanted a night in, a bit of 'me ' time.
She said that Xmas is so busy these days and
she had stuff to do". "Oh" said Santa. What
could that be? he wondered.
Allegra told Santa how she was asked by
Blitzen to take her place this year.

Santa was surprised, but to be honest Blitzen
had been doing her job for a very long time
now and she wasn't quite up to date with all
the mod cons.

Maybe he could find her an office job or maybe in a training capacity. Yes, that was a good idea. He like Allegra and she was very clever with his new gadgets, she had potential.

As they whizzed past the Atlantic Ocean, Unseen beaches and desert islands, he had the idea of a Santa hub, with lots of screens and computers, helping with his deliveries over the Christmas season. Mums and dads could even help with ordering and he'd never get a present wrong again!!! Ooh that was a new project. Maybe Blitzen could help organise this?

In no time at all

Rudolf and co spotted the big old house that
Santa lived in, its red minareted turrets, and
its snowy white tree lined pathway perfect for
the sleigh to take off on! They could see the
swish stable that he had built for them,
centrally heated by a big log fire.
Outside Mrs Santa was waiving madly in
delight that they were back safe and sound
again.
She had been worried and so had Blitzen;
who was a bit downcast.
Was Santa going to be cross with her?

Blitzen and Mrs Santa came to greet them
and all of the elves who had been living it up
with cherry juice, Christmas biscuits and
French bon-bon's.

Blitzen looked sad and ashamed, but she had a nice secret.

All night she'd stayed up and made something really nice for Santa and the reindeer.

"Here you are" said Blitzen. "I'm sorry I wasn't with you, but I think you'll like my Xmas present".

"It's ok" said Santa, "no worries now." Santa told her of his plan and how she would be in charge of the new 'Santa Hub' next year. She was thrilled. A 'Win Win' situation.

Blitzen's surprise

That evening Blitzen was in the toy factory finishing off her presents. She had just finished adding all the sparkly bits and pockets for the new gadgets that Santa had bought.

In popped Allegra full of beans.
'We had a fabulous journey in the new sleigh', she said.
In hopped Raymond, one of the new reindeer, Santa called him Ray, he had a white s shaped flash on his forehead, he was new to sleigh pulling, but to be honest it wasn't so hard once you go the hang of it! He had enjoyed the slight hiccups when things went wrong!

Before you could say star dust, in danced the triplets, Donna, Twinkle and Lucy. They were

very pretty reindeer, and they loved a good
night out with Blitzen when they got a chance.

They started to prance around and sing their
favourite song at this time of the year;
something about Santa coming to town.
All was very merry and bright.
Blitzen was convinced they glowed even more
than usual. She felt lucky to have such
amazing reindeer friends.
She'd made the right decision not to go with
Santa. She should stay home and let the
young ones go next year. They could handle
it.

Santa's Inkling

Santa felt that Elf no 1, or Elfy as he called him in private, deserved a special present this year. He valued his knowledge and his hard work. He could not run the outfit without Elfy who had been his No 1 for a few hundred years now.

In the summer he'd spotted Elfy looking enviously at his friends Snow bike, , and the thought this would be a great idea, and very useful to their whole Christmas operation. The only problem was that they didn't look Christmassy and they were very slow. They also had difficulties with 'taking off' and landing.
However, he knew thought that the clever Elves could adapt things and he was pretty certain that Elfy could change one to suit his needs.

So, he had ordered one from the North pole snow bike catalogue. It was a red one, with white flashes on it.

On the day it arrived Elf was very busy fortunately, so Santa gave it to the other elves secretly to prepare and to paint in a sort of Christmassy way. He felt it needed thrusters, and flashy lights a bit like his Santa Nav. After a week or two, Santa went to see what the elves had done.

The elves had done a great Job, it now had big silver exhaust pipes, flashy lights and a big carrier box to hold gifts. He couldn't wait for Elfy to see it. He wasn't sure how it would perform or how fast it could go, but that was for Elfy to sort out.
They had to hide it in a shed and cover it over with an invisible rug.

They were very pleased with their efforts, but they knew Elfy would probably do more. They couldn't wait for Christmas day to see his face.

Santa sat in his big chair

rocking 'to and fro' in front of the fire.
He'd had turkey, chestnut stuffing, sprouts
and Christmas pudding. He was stuffed. His
new suit would not fit him now!! But thankfully
he had a new star dust one that Blitzen had
made on the elf sewing machine. Red and
glittery with cosmic decorations on it.
He loved the pocket for his Imp phone, and
his new Xmas Imp Watch that Mrs S and the
kids had given him, would be very useful in
case he fell off his seat again!
Of course, the new suit wasn't for' every day'
wear, but it would be for his special trip next
year. It had plenty of room in it to expand! It
was perfect!

Outside, the new reindeer, Rudolf, Allegra,
Donna, Twinkle, Ray and Lucy stood in similar
outfits, sparkling so brightly and glittering in

the moonlight. Their head dresses would keep them warm this year and next.

Mrs S loved her new sparkly apron with Imp phone pocket, and Red-tooth facility, so she could easily keep track of Santa.

The Elves were already thinking of new presents for the children. They were shining up the Nav sleigh to put it safely in the shed till next Christmas Eve.

Blitzen was happy now. She had a new 'special' job for next Christmas.

Santa was pleased that the new Santa Nav had been a success.

Mrs Santa was relieved that all were home safely.
In fact, everyone was happy.

Elfy was beyond happy with his new and amazing snow bike. He would have many more amazing adventures to look forward to. "Roll on next year"! Thought Santa, I just can't wait!

What a 'super dooper', Santa's Nav Journey we had!

Printed in Great Britain
by Amazon